Careers for Creative People

Careers in Animation and Comics

W.L. Kitts

San Diego, CA

© 2020 ReferencePoint Press, Inc.
Printed in the United States

For more information, contact:
ReferencePoint Press, Inc.
PO Box 27779
San Diego, CA 92198
www.ReferencePointPress.com

LIBRARY OF CONGRESS CATALOGING-IN-PUBLICATION DATA

Name: Kitts, W.L., author.
Title: Careers in Animation and Comics/by W.L. Kitts.
Description: San Diego, CA: ReferencePoint Press, Inc., 2020. | Series:
   Careers for Creative People | Includes bibliographical references and
   index. | Audience: Grades 9 to 12. |
Identifiers: LCCN 2018058353 (print) | LCCN 2018060581 (ebook) | ISBN
   9781682826768 (eBook) | ISBN 9781682826751 (hardback)
Subjects: LCSH: Animated films—Vocational guidance—Juvenile literature. |
   Animators—Juvenile literature. | Computer animation—Vocational
   guidance—Juvenile literature. | Comic books, strips, etc.—Vocational
   guidance—Juvenile literature.
Classification: LCC NC1765 (ebook) | LCC NC1765 .K58 2020 (print) | DDC
   741.5023—dc23
LC record available at https://lccn.loc.gov/2018058353

Contents

Growth Faster than a Speeding Bullet

There has never been a better time to have a career in animation or comic books. The increased demand for content in both of these creative fields is fueling tremendous growth. There are more ways to be entertained by shows, movies, video games, and books than ever before—not only online, where the audience has grown exponentially, but also on mobile devices. In fact, as of September 2018, mobile browsing (51.7 percent) had surpassed computer browsing (44.1 percent) worldwide, according to the website Statcounter. In addition to mobile apps, a huge amount of content is needed for streaming channels, publishers, television networks, film studios, and developers specializing in online, virtual reality, and augmented reality games.

That means lots of potential work for comics and animation aficionados who are bursting with creative ideas. They are no longer bound by the interests of the big studios and publishers who traditionally acted as gatekeepers in these industries. In a June 2018 article on the TechCrunch website, Rex Grignon, the chief executive officer of Nimble Collective (a cloud-based animation platform), discussed the impact of these new opportunities. "Now anyone can create a compelling story in their basement and the world will have a chance to see it," he explained. "And if it finds its audience, it can be as big as any studio release. Never before has that been possible."

A mash-up between related industries is also leading to new job opportunities in animation and comics. Popular television shows are becoming video games, and successful video games are becoming television shows. Some comic books feature stories about well-known rock bands. And there has been an explosion of film, television, and video game adaptations of popular comic books.

Traditional literary publishers have also discovered the merit of graphic novels and are actively seeking authors and illustrators to create those works. This adds yet another career option beyond working for comic book publishers. In his online column entitled "Five Trends to Watch in the Comics Business in 2018," Rob Salkowitz of the website ICv2 comments, "A new generation of readers is discovering great graphic works for young, middle-year and young adult audiences in bookstores. Publishers and distributors finally seem to understand how to create and market content for this audience, and it doesn't involve comic stores."

It is clear that animation and comic books cut across age groups, gender, and multiple industries, including publishing, advertising, video games, television, and film. But whether a person is a comic book writer, a movie animator, or a video producer, professionals in the creative fields of animation and comics have a common denominator: each is a storyteller. Whether by pen, by mouse, or by brush, each of these specialists is telling a visual story.

Where Art Meets Technology

The majority of jobs in the animation and comics industries are highly creative. To many people in these fields, work often feels more like play. Being able to create something out of nothing—like a fascinatingly complex imaginary world or a multifaceted character—is both creative and fulfilling.

Although creativity cannot be taught, the skills needed to work in animation and comics can be learned and honed through education and practice. Not all jobs require coursework or degrees, but education can add value to job candidates in these highly competitive fields. Education provides an introduction to the essential digital tools used by people who work in these fields, and it offers an opportunity to sharpen those skills.

Many artists in these industries once developed their stories and sketches using little more than paper and pencil. Some still do their preliminary work that way. But today's tool of choice is

Careers in Animation and Comics

Occupation	Minimum Educational Requirement	2017 Median Pay
Art director	Bachelor's degree	$92,500
Craft and fine artist	No formal educational requirement	$49,160
Editor	Bachelor's degree	$58,770
Film and video editor, and camera operator	Bachelor's degree	$58,210
Multimedia artist and animator	Bachelor's degree	$70,530
Producer and director	Bachelor's degree	$71,620
Writer and author	Bachelor's degree	$61,820

Source: Bureau of Labor Statistics, *Occupational Outlook Handbook*, 2018. www.bls.gov.

the computer. Animation and comics rely heavily on digital technology; therefore, a person seeking a job in one of these fields must be adept at using a variety of digital tools and be up to date on the latest software trends.

Freedom and Flexibility

A person following a creative career path can often create his or her own job. According to 2016 data from the Bureau of Labor Statistics, almost 60 percent of multimedia artists and animators and 64 percent of writers are self-employed. This allows people in the animation and comic book fields to be flexible with their schedules and work from anywhere in the world.

Freelancing is not for everyone, however. Freelancers must find their own work, and they do not receive a regular paycheck every two weeks. They also need good business skills if they are to succeed. Not all creatives are comfortable being an entrepreneur, but for some, the flexibility and freedom that freelancing offers offsets any negatives.

And whether one is a freelancer or an employee, people in creative careers also need to showcase their abilities in order to find work. Making industry connections and marketing their work is crucial, and a portfolio of their best and most recent work is a necessity. Whether drawings, writing samples, a sample comic book, or an animated film reel, a portfolio provides a vivid visual example of work done and ideas yet to be realized.

Creative Collaboration

Although many independent artists and writers work alone (especially freelancers), the comics and animation industries are actually very collaborative. One only has to watch the closing credits on an animated movie to realize this. In a large comic book company, for example, an artist might do only one aspect of the artwork, such as creating the backgrounds or lettering. Plus, when it comes to writing, an editor has a great deal of influence over a writer's text.

Grignon also believes that the increasing ability to collaborate globally will make it both less costly and easier to break into the business for those starting out: "Teams have to collaborate and share their ideas to help a story reach its full potential. Until recently, the connective technology hasn't been up to the task. Now, at last, the cloud makes a lot of those limitations obsolete. It doesn't matter if your teammate is sitting at the next desk or in Seoul, Dublin or Mexico City."

Video Game Animator

What Does a Video Game Animator Do?

The life cycle of a video game, from creation to launch, can be anywhere from three months for a simple mobile game to three years for a full-featured one—and it all starts with an idea. Game designers and developers take that idea and plan the storyline, characters, and the interactive elements. Programmers and artists create the game's code, and concept artists design the game's look along with the characters and backgrounds. And then the animators take over.

Tony Ravo is a video game character animator who has been creating characters for games such as *Assassin's Creed* and *Marvel Super Hero Squad* since 1996. He spoke about his career on the Game Industry Career Guide website:

> Being an animator is a cross between Dr. Frankenstein and an actor. We basically have to animate—which literally means "give life" to—static drawings or [three-dimensional] character models. That's the Dr. Frankenstein part. The actor part is not just moving them around,

At a Glance

Video Game Animator

Minimum Educational Requirements
Bachelor's degree preferred

Personal Qualities
Advanced drawing, digital, and storytelling skills; attention to detail; communication, time-management, organizational, and problem-solving skills

Working Conditions
In an office or from home, dealing with tight deadlines and high pressure

Salary Range
About $40,000 to more than $123,000*

Number of Jobs
Almost 74,000 as of 2016*

Future Job Outlook
Growth of 8 percent through 2026*

*Includes multimedia artists and animators

but giving them personality and purpose so the player cares about the character no matter how large they are on the screen.

Animators collaborate with other artists, including modelers, texture artists, and motion-capture artists. First, the modelers build three-dimensional (3-D) digital frameworks, or skeletons, for the characters, objects, and scenes. This is called rigging. Then, along with texture artists, they do skinning—digitally wrapping the skeletons with two-dimensional textures like skin, fur, and other simulated textures. Finally, using specialized software, the animators bring the skeletons to life through movement, attitude, and behavior. By manipulating light, texture, and color, they also produce depth, which enhances the sense of realism. Sometimes animators are helped by motion-capture artists, who record the movements of real people or animals. Viewing these recordings can help an animator understand how muscles move, for example, and create more authentic-looking characters. This part of the animation process can be time-consuming, so animators often create a library of animations that can be reused for each character or object to save time.

According to Steve Bowler, the lead designer at Phosphor Games and an animator since the mid-1990s, one of the biggest misconceptions about creating video games is that "it's all fun and games." In an interview on the *Lifehacker* blog, he says, "I really enjoy the challenges of making games. It's one of the most mentally stimulating and rewarding fields I've ever worked in. It's also caused me the most anxiety and stress. We work very, very hard. . . . We iterate on something 100 times before it's right. Even if we've done it before."

Bowler says working in this field takes dedication:

Make games, write code, make art, every single day. You don't get to be the best by taking a single class or earning a degree or even landing a single job. . . . If you're not constantly striving to improve yourself and your craft, you're falling behind everyone else who is.

But most importantly, don't go into making games because you love playing games. You have to enjoy the challenge of creating this problem of a game that didn't exist, and then fix that problem by creating that out of nothing.

How Do You Become a Video Game Animator?

Education

It is possible to be hired as a video game animator without any postsecondary education, but the applicant would need both solid art skills and technical know-how. The majority of people in this field have a bachelor's degree specializing in computer graphics, game design, digital art, animation, or illustration. Courses might include 3-D modeling, interactive animation techniques, and artificial intelligence.

Some employers will accept an associate's degree or certificate as long as it includes some combination of art and technology coursework. It is important to enroll in an animation program that focuses on video games; these programs include design and interactive aspects that general animation programs might not.

Learning how to use industry-standard software is essential—and that knowledge can be gained both inside and outside of school. Bowler says, "With the most popular (and most used) game engines now free or very low cost . . . , there's no excuse to not know how to use an engine before you apply [for a job]. Download it. Do the tutorials. Make something."

Education is always valuable, but making something—having something to show prospective employers, even if it is only a personal project—also has value. Bowler agrees, commenting that he "would take a new entry level designer with no degree or 'equivalent experience' who showed their work in creating their own game over someone with a degree who couldn't show their work in a heart-beat."

Video game animators give personality and purpose to characters, objects, and action in every video game. They manipulate light, texture, and color to create a sense of realism or whatever effect the game developer had in mind.

Internships

Many gaming companies offer on-the-job training. And both companies and video game educational programs offer internships. An internship can help an applicant "stand out from the masses," according to the GameDesigning.org article "Animation Internships 10." The article states that "*Internships* are the **best way to get experience** in the video game and film industries if you are starting with none. Real life experience working on real projects with real release dates, with a team of real professionals . . . that looks a lot better than just a degree."

Breaking Into the Business

Mid- to high-level positions in the gaming industry generally require two to four years' experience. But aspiring video game animators right out of school can apply for entry-level jobs. Sometimes it is easier to break into the industry through a smaller game studio. Animators might also freelance to perfect their craft and gain experience while building their portfolio.

A strong portfolio featuring life drawings and movement studies is important for game animators. According to an article that appears on the OnlineDesignTeacher website, the portfolio must also include a show reel of animation projects: "Reels should last about 2-3 minutes and detail the specific contribution the Animator made to the work. Recruiters will look for a variety of genres and styles; walk and run cycles, as well as more fully developed sequences; and, perhaps most important, an ability to portray a character's personality through movement and behaviour."

Self-promotion is an important step in connecting with people in the industry. Animation conferences and video game competitions offer a chance to get one's name and work out into the video game sphere. Many animators also promote their work on their own websites and on industry websites, social media, and online forums. Many game developers watch these spaces for new talent.

Skills and Personality

Video game development requires collaboration. Game animators need to work with a variety of people, including artists, designers, and programmers. Ideas must be communicated clearly, so great communication skills are needed. On the Game Industry Career Guide website, video game character animator Tony Ravo says that coming up with ideas and collaborating with his team are his favorite parts of the job. "It really is awesome when you are brainstorming with creative people and what at first seemed like a small, almost insignificant idea takes life because someone took it and added to it."

Game animators are highly creative, but technical skills are just as important in this job. Animators work with multiple software platforms and digital tools. In addition to having expertise in digital animation techniques, they must be able to draw by hand. In smaller studios, the animators may also be responsible for the rigging and skinning of characters.

People who are looking to be successful in this career need to be detail oriented, well organized, and have effective time-management skills. They also must work well under pressure to solve problems and meet the constant deadlines of launching a game. "Even when you're making a sequel to something you've already made once, there are always new challenges that have to be solved," Bowler says. "In our business it feels like often there are no shortcuts, so personal experience and problem solving are often the best tools of the trade."

On the Job

Employers

The Bureau of Labor Statistics (BLS) groups multimedia artists and animators as one occupational group. In 2016 this group held close to seventy-four thousand jobs. Almost 60 percent were held by self-employed individuals, up by 14 percent from 2014. Eleven percent worked in the motion picture and video sectors, and another 11 percent worked in computer systems and software development.

Jobs in this industry are competitive. Video game animators may find employment with video game companies, software development firms, online game companies, mobile app developers, animation studios, and the entertainment industry. In November 2018, for example, online job boards like Glassdoor and Indeed displayed approximately two hundred job openings for video game animators. Available positions ranged from a senior narrative animator for Sony PlayStation's *God of War* game in Los Angeles, California, to a technical animator job at Nintendo's Retro Studios in Austin, Texas.

Working Conditions

According to the BLS, the majority of people in this field work from home as freelance or contract workers. A smaller group work from corporate offices or studios; often, though, once a game is completed, so are the jobs.

Video game animators generally work a standard workweek. As the launch date approaches, many may work evenings and weekends as well. Game developers are often under intense pressure to create a successful game despite financial and time constraints.

Earnings

According to the BLS, the median annual wage for multimedia artists and animators in May 2017 was more than $70,000. The lowest 10 percent earned less than $40,000, and the highest 10 percent earned over $123,000. Several factors can affect how much a video game animator earns. Those factors include level of experience, area of expertise, and the size of the company.

Opportunities for Advancement

Technology changes constantly in this industry. Animators with knowledge of industry-specific graphics and video production programs and software will have better opportunities to advance. And even though programming and coding skills are not necessary in this job, they may provide an advantage. Plus, many animation skills are transferrable. Video game animators could find opportunities in other industries, such as advertising, television, and film.

What Is the Future Outlook for Video Game Animators?

The BLS reports that jobs for multimedia artists and animators (which include video game animators) are projected to grow 8 percent through 2026. That is another sixty-two hundred jobs and is about as fast as the average for all occupations.

This growth is despite a trend of companies hiring animators overseas to cut costs. However, there has been an increased demand for games both online and on mobile devices. According to the *2018 Essential Facts About the Computer and Video Game Industry* report compiled by the Entertainment Software Association, only 36 percent of video games are played on traditional game consoles.

Also, as processors and graphics continue to evolve, there will be continued demand for games with more realistic-looking images and enhanced experiences such as virtual or augmented reality (AR) like Niantic's *Pokémon Go*. Plus, as AR becomes more affordable, the market will expand further. In July 2017, Orbis Research reported that the AR market will reach almost $285 billion by 2023. All of this indicates a bright future for video game animators.

Find Out More

Gamasutra
303 Second St.
South Tower, Suite 900
San Francisco, CA 94107
website: www.gamasutra.com

Gamasutra is about the art and business of game development. Its website features a blog, articles, job bank, and a place to list contract services.

Game Career Guide
website: www.gamecareerguide.com

This online resource features a job board, online counseling, a place for students to post games, and information about schools and programs for aspiring game designers.

Graphic Artists Guild
31 W. Thirty-Fourth St., Eighth Floor
New York, NY 10001
website: www.graphicartistsguild.org

The Graphic Artists Guild provides advocacy, community, and resources for graphic artists, interactive designers, illustrators, cartoonists, digital artists, animators, web programmers, and developers. Its website offers webinars as well as information on ethics, pricing work, and contracts.

International Game Developers Association (IGDA)
150 Eglinton Ave. E., Suite 402
Toronto, ON
M4P 1E8 Canada
website: www.igda.org

The IGDA is a nonprofit organization that supports game programmers, producers, writers, and artists worldwide through advocacy, community, and resources. The IGDA website also features a career center.

International Web Association
556 S. Fair Oaks Ave., #101–200
Pasadena, CA 91105
website: http://iwanet.org

The International Web Association provides educational and certification standards for web professionals. Its website features information about web certification, education programs, and employment resources.

Web Animator

What Does a Web Animator Do?

Web animators create animations that make websites, video presentations, and mobile apps more fun, more appealing, and more engaging. Some animators are hired to make the Internet more user-friendly, as with the dancing bear that distracts users while they wait for a website to download. Some web animators make educational or marketing videos (called explainer ads) that have moving and changing infographics. Some generate emojis or memes to lighten or personalize social media communication. Some craft special effects, like making it seem as though a car is driving out of a billboard advertisement. Some create animated logos, such as the Google Doodle, to brand a company. Some build game apps, such as Google Games or *Angry Birds*. And some even create wildly popular web series, such as *How It Should Have Ended* or *Simon's Cat*.

Simon Tofield, an award-winning animator, describes his rise to fame in "The Simon's Cat Story," his animated film that appears on YouTube: "Drawing was

At a Glance

Web Animator

Minimum Educational Requirements
Bachelor's degree preferred

Personal Qualities
Creative, advanced digital and storytelling skills; attention to detail; excellent communication, organizational, and time-management skills

Working Conditions
In an office or from home, with constant deadlines

Salary Range
About $40,000 to more than $123,000*

Number of Jobs
Almost 74,000 as of 2016*

Future Job Outlook
Growth of 8 percent through 2026*

*Includes multimedia artists and animators

the only thing I could really do, so I became an animator." Tofield made traditional animated television ads for thirteen years before teaching himself digital animation. "I made my short film about my own cat Hugh trying to get my attention in the morning to be fed." That 2008 black-and-white film propelled Tofield (and his cats) to Internet fame, generating a YouTube channel with almost 5 million subscribers. *Simon's Cat* has since spawned book deals, games, comic strips, toys, and partnerships with Disney and *Sesame Street*.

Not all web animators achieve this level of professional success and fame. Many work behind the scenes creating website banners (which are embedded animated advertisements on webpages) and screen savers (like floating bubbles) that are generated during a computer's hibernation mode. Some web animations, like fading text, hidden menus, or parallax scrolling (where background images move more slowly behind foreground images or text to provide depth), are less noticeable to the average computer or mobile device user, but someone had to create them, and that job usually falls to the web animator. Chris Gannon is an interactive designer who uses animation in his work. In a January 2018 article on the Creative Bloq website, Gannon explains the role of animation in web design: "Animation can play a huge part in making ideas and interfaces easier to understand. . . . In a world where everyone is in a hurry and time is short, animation can convey complex ideas in a short amount of time whilst at the same time engaging and informing."

Although some web animators work alone, collaboration is common. Animator Matthew Cruikshank leads the team of Google Doodlers—the group that creates the company's iconic animated homepage logo feature that commemorates holidays, events, achievements, and people. The group brainstorms regularly to come up with Google Doodle ideas.

Even without the use of words, Google Doodles are known for being expressive. Achieving this result can be challenging. "It's a challenge we relish," Cruikshank explains on the website of the *Guardian* newspaper. "We're aware that we have to make a Doodle global, so we can't use language that wouldn't make sense in one territory, and it almost becomes a series of graphic symbols." Sometimes this requires outside help. For a 2011 Google Doodle commemorating dancer Martha Graham, for instance, the team consulted with the principal dancer of Graham's dance company. She performed for them while they recorded and animated her movements, giving the animated sequence that appeared as the Google Doodle a more authentic feel.

On big projects, it is not uncommon for a web animator to develop a concept, go back to the team for feedback, and then revise it—sometimes more than once. Concepts are often mapped out with a sequence of rough drawings known as a storyboard. Animators can also add dialogue and music to create an animatic, or moving storyboard; this helps them visualize the story, pacing, and timing.

Web animation—or any animation for that matter—can be a slow, painstaking process. According to the *Simon's Cat* website, each second of the show takes between twelve and twenty-five drawings. It takes Tofield two to three months to make an episode, depending on its length, whether it is in color, and how many characters are involved. "I first work on the story idea and then it takes most of that time to get the animation done," he says. "Although we're working on computers, *Simon's Cat*'s all hand-drawn animation. It's made frame-by-frame and it just takes a long time to make each episode."

This is a career that—despite being highly technical—has not lost its creativity. "I'm still drawing all the time filling up sketchbooks with ideas for stories and gags," says Tofield. "I feel really lucky to be doing what I love and it's fantastic to know there's an audience out there waiting to see what *Simon's Cat* gets up to next."

How Do You Become a Web Animator?

Education
A degree is not required for web animation. Aspiring web animators with strong artistic and technical skills and experience in the latest industry-standard animation and graphic design software

Making websites, video presentations, and mobile apps more fun, more appealing, and more engaging is the job of web animators. They must be creative but also have the technical know-how to create products that work on various formats.

may be hired without formal education. However, a bachelor's degree might provide an advantage in this highly competitive industry. There are more people who want to work in web animation than there are jobs.

Students looking for formal education should choose a degree in computer animation, graphic design, or fine arts. Many art institutes and technical schools offer associate's degrees and certificates in programs such as computer animation, web development, web design, and computer programming. A program that offers both an art and technical education would be best, especially if focused on animation. Programs with courses in three-dimensional (3-D) animation, web design, life drawing, and cinematography would be helpful. Programming and coding skills may offer an advantage as well, and web animators might consider obtaining professional certification in various industry-standard software programs.

Internships

Many degree programs and some animation studios offer internships. Internships provide invaluable experience as well as the opportunity to learn about the industry and make connections—often while getting paid.

Internships offer an advantage when it comes to looking for a job. Interns already know what it is like to work in real-world animation. They have practical experience and hands-on technical know-how. For example, Alex Clark Studios, a Los Angeles–based animation studio whose video series *It's Alex Clark* garners 3.4 million YouTube followers, regularly hires interns. On the *Thinking Animation* blog, the studio shares a typical day for its interns: "The first half of the day you'll work on your own PERSONAL Toon Boom [animation software] projects. We will assist you with the goal of elevating your work and understanding of Toon Boom. The second half of the day, you'll be assisting us with art/animation and office tasks."

Breaking Into the Business

A strong portfolio featuring life drawings and movement studies is important for breaking into this industry. It should also include a show reel. In fact, web animators should consider making (and posting on YouTube or other sites) their own web shorts and other work to demonstrate expertise in visual effects and animation software. Generating a following could help attract professional interest or at least demonstrate one's skills and talents.

Skills and Personality

Web animators are both highly creative and technologically forward, and it helps if they can switch back and forth easily between the two sides. They need strong art skills, a good eye for design, storytelling ability, and cinematography skills. In addition, web animators need strong computer skills. They need to be up to date on the latest industry software, and some animators even write their own code.

Web animators need to know both traditional and digital animation techniques. The tools of the web animator's trade include old-fashioned pencil and paper for making preliminary sketches. Most contemporary animators, however, sketch their ideas with specialized computer software, digital pens, and digital paper. They need to be proficient in both two-dimensional animation (used in *The Simpsons*, for example) and 3-D animation (used in *Toy Story*). Some animators also learn the techniques used in stop-motion animation (used in *Chicken Run*).

Great collaboration and communication skills are a must for web animators. They work with a variety of professionals, including artists, designers, and programmers, and ideas need to be communicated clearly.

Students looking to be successful as a web animator also need to be detail oriented and well organized. They require good time-management skills because the industry has constant deadlines.

On the Job

Employers

The Bureau of Labor Statistics (BLS) groups multimedia artists and animators as one occupational group. In 2016 this group held close to seventy-four thousand jobs. Almost 60 percent of these jobs were held by self-employed individuals. Many of these web animators work independently.

Web animators can work for digital or video production companies, web developers, web designers, graphic designers, online game developers, advertising agencies, and marketing companies.

Working Conditions

According to the BLS, the majority of web animators work from home as freelance or contract workers. A smaller group work from corporate offices as employees.

Web animators generally work a standard workweek. However, they tend to work evenings and weekends when they have deadlines. They also experience pressure at work due to deadlines and client expectations.

Earnings
According to the BLS, the median annual wage for multimedia artists and animators in May 2017 was more than $70,000. The lowest 10 percent earned less than $40,000, and the highest 10 percent earned over $123,000.

Opportunities for Advancement
Technology changes constantly in this industry. Web animators can advance if they stay up to date on the latest industry-standard animation software. They might also consider obtaining software certifications to help them stand out and perhaps increase their earnings.

Many animation skills are transferrable. Web animators might find opportunities creating animated content in other industries, such as game development, television, and film.

What Is the Future Outlook for Web Animators?

Jobs for web animators are projected to grow 8 percent through 2026. That is about as fast as the average for all occupations, according to the BLS. This growth is due to an increased demand for enhanced web content and a consumer desire for more realistic images.

There will also be opportunities around virtual and augmented realities—two technologies that are increasing exponentially and have animation applications. Plus, with technological advances like drag-and-drop programs that do not require coding, animations are becoming easier to create. They are becoming faster to download, too, with faster Internet speeds. In "12 Huge Web Design Trends for 2018," an article that appears on the Creative Bloq website, senior design manager Craig Taylor says, "We've witnessed a boom in animated visualisations and an increased appetite for data representation from a 3D perspective. . . . Greater accessibility to new technology will undoubtedly see an increase in the number of designers using animation as a means of storytelling."

In addition, mobile device web browsing has overtaken computer and tablet browsing. This is expected to spike a demand for more content for the smaller mobile format, which is great news for web animators.

Find Out More

Animation Magazine
26500 W. Agoura Rd., Suite 102-651
Calabasas, CA 91302
website: www.animationmagazine.net

Animation Magazine features information about the business, technology, and art of animation and visual effects. The website for this US-based publication includes an international education and career guide, a job center, and lists of animation events and professional development opportunities.

Animation World Network (AWN)
13300 Victory Blvd., Suite 365
Van Nuys, CA 91401
website: www.awn.com

The AWN is an online animation network encompassing more than 151 countries. The AWN site includes a job bank, animated shorts, commercials, trailers, and clips from around the world, and an online magazine dedicated to both the art and business of animation. The site also features an industry database to connect animation and visual effects professionals.

Creative Bloq
website: www.creativebloq.com

Creative Bloq offers information on the latest trends and developments worldwide in art and design to help creative professionals create their best work. The Creative Bloq website is aimed at traditional artists, web designers, graphic designers, 3-D and visual effects artists, and illustrators.

Graphic Artists Guild
31 W. Thirty-Fourth St., Eighth Floor
New York, NY 10001
website: www.graphicartistsguild.org

The Graphic Artists Guild provides advocacy, community, and resources for graphic artists, interactive designers, illustrators, cartoonists, digital artists, animators, web programmers, and developers. Its website offers webinars as well as information on ethics, pricing work, and contracts.

International Web Association
556 S. Fair Oaks Ave., #101-200
Pasadena, CA 91105
website: http://iwanet.org

The International Web Association provides educational and certification standards for web professionals. Its website features information about web certification, education programs, and employment resources.

Producer of Animated Videos

What Does a Producer of Animated Videos Do?

Animation is being used more and more in videos as a way to explain complex topics. In television ads, whiteboard animation videos compare different types of car insurance. In a doctor's office, how-to videos illustrate how to perform breast self-examinations. On YouTube, explainer videos detail how a car's combustion engine works. On learning platforms, a step-by-step animation might show someone how to moonwalk. On media platforms, promotional videos sell products and services. What all of these videos have in common is animated action and a producer who has overseen their creation from concept to completion. Producing animated videos is a great career for anyone who is creative and likes to be in charge.

Jeff Fino, an executive producer whose award-winning animation studio, Wild Brain, produced commercial content for clients such as Coca-Cola and Nike, was interviewed on the Animation World Network (AWN) website. In an article titled "Tips

At a Glance

Producer of Animated Videos

Minimum Educational Requirements
Bachelor's degree preferred

Personal Qualities
Highly creative; extremely organized; excellent communicator; business, management, and leadership skills

Working Conditions
In an office or studio; long hours; high stress; deadline oriented

Salary Range
About $34,000 to $164,000 or more*

Number of Jobs
Almost 135,000 as of 2016*

Future Job Outlook
Growth of 12 percent through 2026*

*Includes producers and directors

on Becoming an Animation Producer," he describes the pace of this type of work:

Producing commercials is much faster than producing cartoons or features. It is swift and it is crazy and it is rewarding, but it *is* eight to twelve weeks. The best sports analogy is the sprint versus the marathon. You have to be well conditioned to do both. Commercials are great because they teach you a variety of styles. On any given day, you could be doing radically different stuff.

Producers wear two hats: an organizational hat and a creative hat. They are the liaison between the executive producer (who oversees the projects at a studio or agency), the client (or investors), and the production team. Producers are responsible for making sure that projects are completed on time and on budget. However, producers are also storytellers. Communicating the client's message in a creative, entertaining, and engaging way is a big part of their job.

During the development, or preproduction, stage, the producer meets with the client to develop a concept for the video. The producer then determines the resources needed, including the hiring of writers, animators, directors, editors, and voice talent. Large productions, like ones that have a mix of live action and visual effects in addition to animation, often have multiple producers supervising different aspects of the project.

Once the concept is conceived, a writer or a team of writers develop a script. The producer reviews the script and offers feedback. After the script is approved, the producer works with the storyboard artist to plan the story visually. This includes creating the characters, background, and a list of shots that will go into creating each scene. A digital moving version of the story, called an animatic, is created to help plot the pacing of the story. Dialogue and sound are often added as well to give the producer an idea of what the finished video will look like. The animatic also serves as a reference for the production team, which will create the actual video.

The different shots will be edited together to create the final product in postproduction. Depending on the size of the studio or the project, sometimes producers do the editing themselves. Music, sound effects, and special effects will also be added at this point. Producers also oversee marketing and distribution of the video, both domestically and internationally if applicable.

This results-oriented job fosters a high sense of achievement and creative satisfaction. The producer is the face of a project. Because he or she has a high degree of creative input (and thus creative control), the producer often gets the credit (or blame) for the quality of the project.

How Do You Become a Producer of Animated Videos?

Education

Producers of animated videos do not need a degree, but most obtain a bachelor's degree in writing, journalism, or communications. Some producers also complete degrees in either business or arts management. Courses in animation and editing in industry-standard software are also a plus.

A background in animation is required, but according to Mark Medernach, an executive producer at Duck Soup, a video animation studio, it is not the most important requirement. As he explains on the AWN website, "If someone has a strong animation background, that is a real plus, but organization is the biggest thing. I cannot stress that enough. It is a people business. The more people skills you have, the better off you will be."

Internships

Some production studios or agencies offer internship programs. Internships are a great way to get experience, cultivate connections, and learn not only about the animation video production process but also the animation industry.

On any given day, an animation video production intern might be meeting with a client, working on a storyboard, or editing a video—all valuable and professional experience that could lead to a paid position. When applying for a job, an internship could set an aspiring producer apart from others.

Breaking Into the Business

The position of producer is not an entry-level job. Most producers work their way up from a production assistant or even an artist or writer. Those with experience in video production, particularly in animation and editing, have an advantage when breaking into this profession, as do those with related skills from film, television, or theater production. Aspiring producers also need to know the production process, understanding how each stage comes together to create the final project. Experience in both management and project coordination is also an asset.

Fino cautions aspiring producers not to expect to start at the top:

> Animation more than many businesses requires you to do a bit of an apprenticeship to learn the process. It does not matter if you are an artist or a producer. You have to prove yourself. If you are a producer, show you have the wherewithal to make a highly collaborative process work. You in essence become one link in that chain, and you have to prove that you are strong with the other links. The good side to that is that your talents are recognized quickly and your value is judged pretty fast. Good people can rise up through the ranks in relatively short order.

A strong portfolio is essential for prospective producers. It should include a show reel of any animated projects they have worked on—even those they may have created in high school. A portfolio needs to communicate the abilities of the aspiring producers so they stand out in this crowded industry.

Skills and Personality

Producers are project managers as well as visionaries. They need to be highly organized; time-management skills are of utmost importance. Projects must come in on schedule and on budget—without sacrificing creativity. Producers need to be able to envision the entire project and calculate the resources, staffing, and funding needed to execute the client's vision. If something goes wrong, producers also need to quickly solve problems and make decisions.

In addition, producers need leadership skills. They need to build, lead, and motivate their teams. They work with everyone—investors, clients, artists, directors, and voice actors—so excellent communication skills are a must, especially when communicating their vision. Good business and financial skills are needed as well because producers negotiate project funding.

Experience with animation is useful, but it is not the most important quality for a producer of animated videos. When looking to hire a producer, Fino says, he takes experience into account but also looks for someone who can adapt and learn quickly: "I think intelligence, organization and enthusiasm are all great qualities that a producer should have. Animation is a bit more specialized. It helps to have some experience, but if you find somebody who is exceptionally smart and enthusiastic about what they are doing, with the proper amount of instruction you can make them into a great producer."

On the Job

Employers

The Bureau of Labor Statistics (BLS) groups producers with directors in the same occupational category. This category includes producers of animated videos as well as producers and directors of other works. According to the BLS, this group held close to 135,000 jobs in 2016. More than sixty jobs were listed for producers of animated videos on the online job board Indeed in November 2018. Jobs ranged from a video producer for Aya Healthcare in San Diego, California, to a digital media producer for Amazon in Seattle, Washington.

Producers of animated videos work in a variety of fields. Six percent work for advertising and public relations companies. Twenty percent work in radio and television broadcasting. The largest share, approximately 30 percent, work in film and video. Sixteen percent of producers identify as self-employed. Others work in the performing arts, sports, and other fields.

Working Conditions

Producers of animated videos generally work for production studios or agencies. Producing is a high-stress job because of deadlines, budget constraints, and the pressure of keeping multiple parties satisfied. When deadlines are looming, it is not unusual for a producer to work evenings, weekends, or even holidays.

Earnings

According to the BLS, the median annual wage for producers and directors in May 2017 was $71,620. The lowest 10 percent in this category earned less than $34,000. The highest 10 percent earned over $164,000. The highest salaries for this group occurred in the advertising, public relations, and related industries, earning more than $90,000 annually.

Opportunities for Advancement

As producers of animated videos gain reputations for highly creative and quality work, other opportunities may open for them. They can progress to overseeing larger projects. Plus, many of their skills are transferrable to animated film and television productions or even live-action or hybrid projects.

Increasing one's skills can also ensure more opportunities to advance in this field. As with most careers that have a technology component, staying up to date with the latest animation trends, software, and technological advances can also help.

What Is the Future Outlook for Producers of Animated Videos?

The BLS reports that opportunities for producers in general will grow faster than average for all occupations. It projects 12 percent growth through 2026. That translates into 16,500 more jobs.

The projected increase is due to an expected demand, both domestic and foreign, for US-produced film and television shows as well as content for Internet platforms. And although this is a highly competitive field, the expected explosion in demand for video content will likely lead to more jobs for producers of animated videos.

Find Out More

Animation Magazine
26500 W. Agoura Rd., Suite 102–651
Calabasas, CA 91302
website: www.animationmagazine.net

Animation Magazine features information about the business, technology, and art of animation and visual effects. The website for this US-based publication includes an international education and career guide, a job center, and lists of animation events and professional development opportunities.

Animation World Network (AWN)
13300 Victory Blvd., Suite 365
Van Nuys, CA 91401
website: www.awn.com

The AWN is an online animation network encompassing more than 151 countries. The AWN website includes a job bank, animated shorts, commercials, trailers, and clips from around the world, and *AnimationWorld Magazine*, an online publication dedicated to both the art and business of animation worldwide. This site also features an industry database to connect animation and visual effects professionals.

Producers Guild of America (PGA)
8530 Wilshire Blvd., Suite 400
Beverly Hills, CA 90211
website: www.producersguild.org

The PGA is a nonprofit organization that promotes the interests of producers in film, television, and new media. The PGA site offers mentoring opportunities, job boards, and online articles about the industry.

Storyboard Artist

What Does a Storyboard Artist Do?

A storyboard artist is one part artist and one part storyteller. With the aid of computer software, these talented professionals use their drawing skills to create a visual story for commercial videos, television, video games, and movies. Storyboarders sketch out the story scene by scene, shot by shot, in sequential panels on what is known as a storyboard.

Storyboarders sometimes start with just an idea or concept, but other times they work with an existing script. Often, they will add dialogue and music to their boards to create an animatic. An animatic is a rough moving version of the storyboard that helps others visualize the story. A board also helps with timing and pacing as well as plotting complex scenes like car chases.

Lauren Walsh, a game design artist, likens storyboarding to doing a rough sketch of the finished product. She says on GameDesigning.org, "It is in this 'sketch' phase when an artist can explore many different concepts, themes, environments and storytelling tools as they convey their idea to the team. Making changes to a

At a Glance

Storyboard Artist

Minimum Educational Requirements
Bachelor's degree preferred

Personal Qualities
Advanced drawing, digital, and storytelling skills; great attention to detail; excellent communication skills

Working Conditions
In an office or from home, with tight deadlines

Salary Range
About $40,000 to more than $210,000*

Number of Jobs
Almost 74,000 as of 2016*

Future Job Outlook
Growth of 8 percent through 2026*

*Includes multimedia artists and animators

simple storyboard before devoting precious time and resources to an idea is much easier and cost effective."

Storyboards are also used to communicate the story to the clients and investors who fund the production, the writers and animators who flesh out the story, and the directors who plan the shots or scenes. Boards also serve as a reference for the production team, helping with camera placement, lighting, backgrounds, and characters. Storyboards are created for projects that are live action, animated, or a mix of both.

Larger productions sometimes have more than one storyboard artist. In those instances, the storyboarders must copy each other's style to ensure consistent boards. With video game productions, storyboarders sometimes work on more than one level of a game, so they need to be cognizant of the visual continuity of the story.

Storyboard artists work closely with the producer and director to edit a story, which involves adding, deleting, and rearranging scenes. On *Valerie's Blog*, Pixar storyboard artist Valerie LaPointe describes the collaborative aspect of storyboarding in a February 2018 post:

> When you are actually storyboarding a sequence, you get feedback initially from the Director and then pitch to the entire team, who also give feedback and ideas. Then you redo it and fix it according to what the Director has in mind. You also attend brainstorm meetings: coming up with ideas/gags or discussing ways to make the story or characters work better. It is a back and forth from big teamwork to solitary work in your office.

Just as good writing requires lots of rewriting, storyboarding, LaPointe notes, also entails plenty of revision. The difference is that writers usually revise their work by starting at the beginning and working their way through to the ending. Storyboarding does not work that way. "It is a crazy, whack-a-doodle process that is not linear," says LaPointe. "We spend ages going back and forth, redoing things in a non-linear process to end up with a very linear narrative story. It's the creative process every day."

How Do You Become a Storyboard Artist?

Education

Although a bachelor's degree is not required, most storyboard artists do have degrees in animation. Others obtain a degree in fine arts, illustration, graphic design, or even film.

Some artists enroll in digital arts, illustration, or animation programs. These programs typically offer courses in visual storytelling, character design, editing, and digital illustration. Animation programs also focus on storyboarding, film techniques, conceptualization, special effects, and the use of sound.

Internships

Some educational programs will help place students in internships. This allows them to not only get valuable experience but also make connections with people in the industry.

Eric Bravo, the creator of *The Storyboard Room* animation blog, did three internships while he was in college, including internships with the mega animation studios Nickelodeon and DreamWorks. These internships led to Bravo creating his own cartoon short. He shares his secret to obtaining these coveted positions on the Cartoon Brew website: "Most students apply for internships during the summer, which makes these programs very competitive, especially for the highly sought out studios. If you want to better your chances, apply during the off-seasons (Fall/Spring semester) and take some classes at your college during the summer instead."

Bravo's first internship was with Warner Bros. Records. Even though it was not in animation, Bravo felt it helped him snag the other two internships. "Once you have a major studio on your résumé, no matter the industry it is, it will open more doors and help you land internships at other major studios, including animation studios."

Breaking Into the Business

Storyboarding is not an entry-level job. Most jobs require two to four years' experience in digital design along with strong drawing skills. However, if a person is extremely talented artistically, she

A storyboard artist sketches out a story scene by scene, shot by shot, in sequential panels. Storyboarders are part artist and part storyteller.

or he can obtain an artist's entry-level job. Many storyboarders start out as animators or layout artists, who draw or create backgrounds from the storyboards.

A strong portfolio is a necessity. The portfolio should demonstrate an ability to tell stories visually with drawings. This could include storyboards done as school projects, for internships, and for freelance or other jobs. It also helps to show boards for different media; for example, for film and for video games. Alex Williams, the head of animation for Escape Studios, says today's portfolios are online links. In *Skwigly*, a British online animation magazine, he asserts that "DVDs and paper portfolios are history. Your reel should be easy to find; hosted at your blog or website."

Professionals in the field also suggest that aspiring storyboard artists post their work on art sites and social media. It can help build a following, and producers and directors often check out these forums for new talent.

It also helps storyboarders to study films. In an August 2018 article in the British newspaper the *Telegraph*, storyboard artist Simon Duric encouraged storyboarders to watch movies to assess the director's camera shots and angles, the actors' facial expressions and body postures, and the overall story. "Watch everything. Look at paintings. Photography. Immerse yourself in moving images. I see watching a film as homework, which is both a blessing and a curse. Especially if it's a bad film."

Skills and Personality

Storyboard artists are highly creative. Not only do they need to be effective and engaging storytellers, but they also need advanced drawing skills to tell their stories visually and clearly. They need to know how to draw sequentially, pay attention to detail, and be able to adapt to other artists' styles. They also should be familiar with digital storytelling and have knowledge of industry-standard software for storyboards, graphics, and editing.

Storyboarders need to be film literate. They need to understand composition, angles, camera shots, editing choices, and lighting techniques. Being familiar with acting also helps when drawing characters, especially when communicating their emotions.

Storyboard artists need great communication skills. Although they most often work alone, they need to be able to present their vision to clients, producers, directors, writers, and animators. They also need to be able to take constructive criticism because they will constantly be revising their boards based on other people's feedback.

On the Job

Employers

The Bureau of Labor Statistics (BLS) groups multimedia artists and animators as one occupational group. This includes storyboard artists. In 2016 this group occupied almost seventy-four thousand jobs. Almost 60 percent of these jobs were held by self-employed individuals. Eleven percent worked in the motion picture and video sectors, and 4 percent worked in advertising and public relations. Others worked for computer and software companies.

Storyboarders have opportunities in many industries. Jobs may be found at advertising agencies; video, movie, animation, and video game studios; television networks; and specialty and live-streaming channels. In November 2018, for instance, nearly two hundred jobs related to storyboard artists were posted on Indeed, an online job board. A job listed at the Nickelodeon Animation Studio in Burbank, California, was for a full-time storyboarder for the animated television series *SpongeBob SquarePants*. Another was for the Multi Image Group (MIG), a communications company in Boca Raton, Florida. MIG was looking for a storyboard artist for animation videos for corporate events and marketing campaigns.

Working Conditions

According to the BLS, the majority of storyboard artists work from home as freelance or contract workers. Others work in corporate offices or studios.

Storyboard artists generally work a standard workweek. However, when deadlines loom, many work evenings and weekends as well. As Duric explains, "Sometimes my work will involve creating boards for pitches: showing investors and producers what a project could be. It can involve tight deadlines, many late nights and lots and lots of drawing."

The late nights are often balanced by extended periods of downtime while other team members review the work. But then the work picks up again when the storyboarders are asked to make changes. It is common for storyboarders to redo their boards multiple times to incorporate the production team's suggestions. LaPointe says, "You come up with, literally, thousands of ideas and thoughts that never get used. . . . You also have to be okay with putting your heart into something one minute, and then having it cut and rearranged in the next. It's not for the faint of heart."

Earnings

According to the BLS, the median annual wage for multimedia artists and animators in May 2017 was more than $70,000. The lowest 10 percent earned less than $40,000, and the highest 10 percent earned over $123,000. Many of the larger animation and film studios pay even more. For example, Glassdoor, an online job and recruiting company, reports that the average salary for a storyboard artist at Pixar in January 2018 was over $210,000.

Opportunities for Advancement

Storyboard artists can advance in this industry by staying up to date on all the latest graphics and animation software. They can also learn about film and television production. This could help them move to positions like story supervisor, producer, or director. As LaPointe explains in her blog, "Being a Story Artist definitely gives you skills to direct, as it prepares you for so many other aspects of that job, and could open opportunities to direct even at other studios. Most of Pixar's directors have come from the Story or Animation Department."

What Is the Future Outlook for Storyboard Artists?

Jobs for storyboard artists are projected to grow 8 percent through 2026. That is about as fast as the average for all occupations, according to the BLS. This is due to an increased demand for web, mobile, and streaming content.

Storyboarding is a very competitive industry. Some companies in this field hire overseas artists to save money. However, artists who specialize in a particular storyboard or in cutting-edge software will have the best opportunities.

Find Out More

Animation Magazine
26500 W. Agoura Rd., Suite 102-651
Calabasas, CA 91302
website: www.animationmagazine.net

Animation Magazine features information about the business, technology, and art of animation and visual effects. The website for this US-based publication includes an international education and career guide, a job center, and lists of animation events and professional development opportunities.

Animation World Network (AWN)
13300 Victory Blvd., Suite 365
Van Nuys, CA 91401
website: www.awn.com

The AWN is an online animation network encompassing more than 151 countries. The AWN website includes a job bank, AWNtv (animated shorts, commercials, trailers, and clips from around the world), and *AnimationWorld Magazine*, an online publication dedicated to both the art and business of animation worldwide. The site also features an industry database to connect animation and visual effects professionals.

Computer Graphics World
620 W. Elk Ave.
Glendale, CA 91204
website: www.cgw.com

Computer Graphics World is a digital magazine that covers the latest news and technologies for the animation, film, visual effects, and game industries. Its website also includes blog posts, videos, and portfolio samples.

Graphic Artists Guild
31 W. Thirty-Fourth St., Eighth Floor
New York, NY 10001
website: www.graphicartistsguild.org

The Graphic Artists Guild provides advocacy, community, and resources for graphic artists, interactive designers, illustrators, cartoonists, digital artists, animators, web programmers, and developers. Its website offers webinars as well as information on ethics, pricing work, and contracts.

Visual Effects Animator

What Does a Visual Effects Animator Do?

When the visual effects team was trying to figure out how to make their animated dragon fly for HBO's *Game of Thrones*, it used a frozen chicken to study flight mechanics. As Sven Martin, the visual effects supervisor at Pixomondo, recalls on the Thrillist website, "I forced our animators and riggers to play with the wings to understand the natural restrictions and the anatomy of a real wing. Peeling off the skin to one side to reveal the muscle layout was very helpful . . . , even though it was a little disgusting." The team also did a bit of role-playing to nail down how the dragons might move. Martin says, "I still remember the animator and myself playing the two chained dragons down in a dungeon, struggling against a rope held by our producer."

This is a typical day in the life of a visual effects (VFX) animator. Working together with other specialists, the animator creates a wide range of visually stunning effects for both characters and backgrounds. Although VFX animators are most known for their work on television or film, they work in many other fields. They create computer-generated animations and special effects for animation studios; video game, mobile device, and social media developers; video producers; streaming platforms; web designers; graphic design firms; and advertising agencies.

The work of a VFX animator takes place during the postproduction phase of a project—after the footage has been shot. The animator consults with others involved in the project about the types of effects they envision. In a movie or video game, special effects might include explosions or an advancing invasion of aliens. In an advertising campaign, they might include a talking baby or singing and dancing vegetables in a refrigerator.

Nathaniel Hubbell, a video game special effects artist who worked on games like *Assassin's Creed* and *X-Men*, describes his job on the Game Industry Career Guide website: "What I always tell people is: 'I make anything that moves that isn't a character.' Anything from sparkles to explosions to rippling water to blinking buttons in a menu. The art I make can be simple and subtle, like a couple of moving clouds in the background. Or it can be complex and flashy, like all the superpowers in a superhero game. There's a lot of variety!"

It is up to the VFX animator to figure out the best way to make the effects happen. That process usually begins with basic sketches, either drawn by hand or on a computer. The sketches provide an idea of the basic look and feel of the effects that will eventually be developed in far more detail. The sketches are shared with the director and sometimes other individuals who are working on the project. Based on their feedback, the artist might make changes (often, more than once) to more closely align with the project goals. Once the sketches are approved, the animator creates three-dimensional (3-D) models of the action, characters, and scenes. Using specialized animation software, the VFX animator incorporates light, texture, and color to attain a depth that makes images appear to pop off the screen. Once the effects are completed, they are added to the film footage. And if they are done precisely and artistically, they will be seamless.

Being a VFX animator is a rewarding job that requires both creativity and technical skill. On the Pixelsmithstudios website,

Jason Keyser, a VFX animator at Riot Games, describes what he loves most about his job: "It's always super satisfying seeing something I worked on go out to players, and reading their comments on the forums. I really get a kick out of other people enjoying something I created."

This job also requires passion and dedication. Keyser offers advice for aspiring VFX animators:

> This isn't an industry of practicality. If you want the safe route, don't go into entertainment. If you're going for a job in TV, film, or games, go all in. Dedicate yourself to developing your skills. Don't hold back. . . . Sure, it's competitive, but that shouldn't be a problem for someone who is really excited and passionate about doing the work. It's so rewarding. It's so worth it. Just keep going and never stop. Then you won't have any regrets.

How Do You Become a Visual Effects Animator?

Education

Although it is possible for a person with strong art talent and advanced technical skills in the latest VFX industry-standard software to be hired without formal education, most VFX animators have degrees. Animation is an extremely competitive industry, and a bachelor's degree can provide an advantage. Many VFX animators obtain degrees in animation, computer animation, visual effects, or film and video. Coursework in computer programming may be helpful as well.

Art institutes and technical schools offer associate's degrees and certificates in programs such as animation, special effects, and film. A program that offers both an art and a technical education would be the best fit, especially if focused on animation. Programs with courses in 3-D animation, special effects, and cinematography would also be helpful.

Internships

Many educational programs offer internships. Internships provide invaluable experience as well as the opportunity to learn about the industry and make connections. Many of the larger animation studios offer paid internships of varying lengths and with different areas of emphasis. According to the Pixar website, for instance, an internship there would include working directly with company employees; taking part in company-wide events, screenings, and lectures; and participating in the company's social and civic programs.

Breaking Into the Business

Although advanced positions may require two to five years of experience, this is not always required for an entry-level job as a VFX animator. Experience can provide an advantage, however. Certain skills and knowledge are important for those who want to work in VFX animation—and some of this expertise can only be gained through experience. "Basic color theory, composition, painting, modeling, texturing, and animation are all essential," says Hubbell. "You'll also want to know about rigging, shaders, physics simulation, and as much scripting/coding as you can manage. You don't need to be an expert in all these areas, but you'll want to have a decent practical grasp on them."

A strong portfolio featuring life drawings and movement studies is also important for breaking into this industry. Hubbell recommends that aspiring VFX animators create a show reel of short animations demonstrating various visual effects. "Learn to make fire, water, clouds/smoke, explosions, lightning/electricity, and motion trails," says Hubbell. "Those six things are especially common tasks for effects artists, so they're good to have in your repertoire." It is also important to demonstrate expertise in animation software and basic art skills. "For the software side, grab a game engine and just start playing with it," Hubbell advises. Many are free or, at least, not very expensive. He continues: "Anytime you can't figure something out, look for online tutorials. For the art side, do drawings or paintings of natural phenomena from observation."

Conferences and self-promotion can also enhance one's chances of getting into the business. At conferences, aspiring

VFX animators try to create believable scenes in television, movies, and video games. For a scene like this one from HBO's *Game of Thrones*, VFX animators drew sketches, studied chicken anatomy, created 3D models, and even engaged in role playing.

VFX animators can make connections with producers and directors that might lead to job offers. VFX animators also should promote their animation on their own websites and on social media. They should also post their work on industry websites and online forums because animation industry professionals often search for new talent on these sites.

Skills and Personality

VFX animators work with a variety of people. Therefore, they need to be able to work cooperatively, and they need to have good communication skills. Because most projects are organized around deadlines, strong organization and time-management skills are also essential.

VFX animators need to be skilled both creatively and technologically. They require strong art skills and the ability to understand the effects of color, texture, and light. Plus, their computer skills need to be continuously updated to reflect the latest industry standards.

Being able to solve problems is another necessary skill. "Very often you'll be assigned something you've never done before," explains Hubbell. "A waterfall that flows up? An exploding star?

A cloak made of starlight? A dust storm that's alive? If you enjoy tackling weird, unpredictable challenges, this is an exciting area to be in."

On the Job

Employers

The Bureau of Labor Statistics (BLS) groups multimedia artists and animators as one occupational group. This includes VFX animators. In 2016 this group held close to seventy-four thousand jobs. Almost 60 percent of this group identified as being self-employed. Eleven percent worked in the motion picture and video sectors, and 4 percent worked in advertising and public relations. Others find jobs in a variety of computer-related fields.

VFX animators typically work for animation studios (film, television, and video), video game studios, web designers, advertising or marketing agencies, and graphic design companies. Most of the animation studios are found in larger metropolitan areas. California has a large proportion of studios, especially in cities like Los Angeles and San Francisco.

Working Conditions

The BLS shows that the majority of VFX animators work from home as freelancers or do contract work on-site. Others work from corporate offices or studios as employees.

VFX animators generally work a standard workweek. However, when there are deadlines, which there are many, they may also work evenings and weekends.

Earnings

According to the BLS, the median annual wage for multimedia artists and animators (a group that includes VFX animators) in May 2017 was more than $70,000. The lowest 10 percent earned less than $40,000, and the highest 10 percent earned over $123,000.

Recruiter sites like Glassdoor report that many of the larger animation and film studios, such as Disney and DreamWorks, pay even higher salaries. Glassdoor names San Francisco as one of the top three cities for VFX animation jobs. As an article on the All Art Schools website explains, "Thanks to the flood of high-paying tech jobs in the area, animator salaries are equally competitive; the San Francisco–based animator earns one of the highest salaries in the country."

Opportunities for Advancement

Animation technology changes constantly. VFX animators can progress in this field if they stay up to date on industry-standard software.

VFX animation skills are somewhat transferable to other animation-based industries. A VFX animator could potentially find opportunities doing animation for the web or mobile devices, for example.

> ## What Is the Future Outlook for Visual Effects Animators?

Jobs for VFX animators are projected to grow 8 percent through 2026. That is about as fast as the average for all occupations, according to the BLS. This is due to an increased demand not only for media content for the web, mobile apps, and streaming platforms but also for more realistic images in videos, games, and movies as well as on television.

However, this is a very competitive industry. And some companies in this field hire overseas artists to save money. A VFX animator can counteract these negatives by getting good experience, creating a strong portfolio, and developing a working knowledge of the latest industry technology.

> ## Find Out More

Animation Magazine
26500 W. Agoura Rd., Suite 102–651
Calabasas, CA 91302
website: www.animationmagazine.net

Animation Magazine features information about the business, technology, and art of animation and visual effects. The website for this US-based publication includes an international education and career guide, a job center, and lists of animation events and professional development opportunities.

Animation World Network (AWN)
13300 Victory Blvd., Suite 365
Van Nuys, CA 91401
website: www.awn.com

The AWN is an online animation network encompassing more than 151 countries. The AWN website includes a job bank, animated shorts, commercials, trailers, and clips from around the world and an online magazine dedicated to both the art and business of animation worldwide. The site also features an industry database to connect animation and visual effects professionals.

Cinefex
website: www.cinefex.com

Cinefex is a magazine focused on cinematic visual effects. Its website features blog posts and interviews with VFX professionals.

Creative Bloq
website: www.creativebloq.com

Creative Bloq offers information on the latest trends and developments worldwide in art and design to help creative professionals create their best work. The Creative Bloq website is aimed at traditional artists, web designers, graphic designers, and 3-D and VFX artists and illustrators.

Graphic Artists Guild
31 W. Thirty-Fourth St., Eighth Floor
New York, NY 10001
website: www.graphicartistsguild.org

The Graphic Artists Guild provides advocacy, community, and resources for graphic artists, interactive designers, illustrators, cartoonists, digital artists, animators, web programmers, and developers. Its website offers webinars as well as information on ethics, pricing work, and contracts.

Comic Book Writer

Comic book writers do not think like other people. They think in chunks—or, to be more specific, in panels. When they tell a story, it must take place one piece at a time. Squeezing too much action into each panel does not work. "Spider-Man can't jump off a rooftop, swing across the street and also punch Doc Ock in the same panel. You need to break it up into several," says Scott Aukerman, the writer of *Secret Wars Journal* and *Deadpool*. And that is not easy to do. Aukerman continues in an interview on the website of *Fast Company* magazine: "The thing I struggled most with, in these short stories, is trying to fit too much dialogue into a panel, and too many panels into a page. It can be difficult to tell a satisfying story with a beginning, middle, and end, in that short amount of time."

But that is exactly what comic book writers strive to do. They write for a distinctive format that features a combination of images and words that is typically only thirty-two pages long. Lengthier forms exist, like graphic novels, where writers can explore extended

At a Glance

Comic Book Writer

Minimum Educational Requirements
Bachelor's degree optional

Personal Qualities
Creative; great writing and communication skills; attention to detail; ability to meet deadlines

Working Conditions
Usually in a home office, with lots of computer time and long hours when facing deadlines

Salary Range
About $30,000 to more than $118,000,* with a few earning millions

Number of Jobs
More than 131,000 as of 2016*

Future Job Outlook
Growth of 8 percent through 2026*

*Includes writers and authors

plotlines and develop characters more fully. Regardless, writers need to take the somewhat constrained format into consideration when writing for this unique art form. Taran Killam, creator of *The Illegitimates*, a comic about James Bond's illegitimate children, says writing for comics is different from other writing. In an online interview with *Fast Company*, he offers advice to other comic book writers: "Get to the point. Cut as quickly and clearly as you can to the meat of the story. . . . A character's posture or placement of an object . . . can help your story more often than three pages of dialogue."

Comic book writers create all sorts of stories. Superhero comics tend to get the most attention, but genres such as romance, science fiction, and horror are also common. So are autobiographical or memoir comics, some of which deal with serious themes like cancer, sexuality, and abuse.

All writing, including for comic books, begins with an idea. Even if they are not illustrating the story, most comic book writers do rough sketches showing what action and dialogue will take place in each panel as the story progresses. This helps writers hone their ideas.

Stan Lee (who died in November 2018) is perhaps the world's greatest known comic book writer. He created (and cocreated) some of Marvel's most iconic comic book characters, including Spider-Man, Iron Man, the Hulk, the Fantastic Four, and the X-Men. During a preretirement interview with *Inc.* magazine, Lee explained his process:

> I sit down with a pencil and paper at my desk, and I think about what I can do that hasn't been done before. If I can't think of a new superpower, I try to think of a new quality that a character might have. Maybe this character has a certain ability that's given him nothing but grief. Thinking up stories is easy. Thinking up the characters is easy. It's finding a way to make it something that people have never seen before—that's what's difficult. It's also what's the most fun.

Education

Postsecondary education is not always required for a career as a comic book writer. There are very few dedicated comic book writing programs. The ones that do exist (mostly online) include courses on scripting, formatting, and pacing stories. Still, most writers would be helped by having an associate's or a bachelor's degree, especially if they want to work for a comic book publisher. Competition for these jobs is high; a degree could provide an advantage. Among degrees that would be most valuable are English, journalism or communications, creative writing, or entertainment writing.

Internships

Comic book publishers like DC Comics and Marvel offer internships. Obtaining one of these coveted positions is a great way for a comic book writer to get his or her work noticed. And even though internships may not pay a salary, they provide great connections. Jeremy Melloul of *Creator at Large*, a comic book industry blog, says many comic book creators started out as interns. Melloul interviewed intern Peter Holmstrom about the advantages of an internship. Interning, Holmstrom says, is a "testing ground allowing you to get hands-on experience so you'll know what you're getting into before you spend a bunch of time/money on a degree. Or pursuing a job you'd rather not have."

Breaking Into the Business

Some comic book writers get their start through self-publishing, which can lead to being picked up by a traditional publisher. Writers can also post their work on websites and blogs in hopes of being discovered. In "How to Become a Freelance Writer for Marvel and DC," an article that appears on the Pen & the Pad website, writer Carl Hose encourages aspiring writers to make use of comic-centered websites and blogs. He notes that "websites like these are scouting grounds for Marvel, DC and other comic book companies." Writers can also send sample scripts to publishers.

Many writers attend writing conferences and comic-specific events such as Comic-Con, an international entertainment and comic book convention. Writers can meet editors and publishers, who often accept writing samples. The Scripts & Scribes website advises aspiring writers to do whatever it takes to get noticed— and be persistent:

> It sounds like a catch-22 where you can't get a job without having credits and you can't get credits if they won't give you a job, but it's not hopeless. Go to comic book conventions and introduce yourself to the industry professionals. Make contacts and keep writing and submitting your material to whoever you can find that will read it. You simply have to be persistent and really work at it. It is a career after all and not simply a paid hobby.

That said, comic book writers traditionally have had a harder time breaking into the industry than comic book artists. Writer-artist Jason Thibault offers a work-around on his blog, jasonthibault.com: "There's always room for good writing, and a lot of publishers will still accept writing submissions," says Thibault. "But conventional wisdom says to partner up with an artist if you can. An editor is more likely to read your words if [they are] already on a sequential page."

Skills and Personality

The most important skills for a comic book writer are generating original ideas and communicating those ideas in writing. Clear writing, spelling, and grammar do matter when trying to convey an idea to a publisher.

Writers also need to know the language of comic books. They need to know their audience and be able to write in a way that hooks the reader intellectually and emotionally.

They also need good organizational and time-management skills. These will help them meet deadlines. Not observing timelines can affect a writer's reputation and ability to obtain repeat work.

On the Job

Employers

The Bureau of Labor Statistics (BLS) includes comic book writers under the occupational category of writers and authors. In 2016 this group made up 131,200 jobs in the United States.

Many comics are produced by large comic book publishers such as DC or Marvel, which are generally created by a team of writers and artists. At independent, creator-owned publishers like Image Comics, the comics are created by the writers and artists themselves. Often, the writer is also the artist.

Comics are also created by freelance writers. According to the BLS, 64 percent of this occupational group identified as self-employed.

Working Conditions

Freelance writers generally work from their own homes or offices. Writers who work for a publisher typically work in an office environment and observe a standard workweek. Of course, all writers put in long hours when up against deadlines. And most spend the bulk of their time sitting in front of a computer.

Earnings

According to the BLS, in 2017 the median annual wage for writers and authors was approximately $62,000 per year. The lowest 10 percent of this occupational category earned less than $30,000, and the highest 10 percent earned more than $118,000.

Unless they are salaried employees with a publisher, comic book writers often get paid by the project or page. The Creator Resource website surveys comic professionals annually. It reports that comic writers earned $35 to $240 per page in 2017.

The most successful comic book creators often become celebrities and have the potential to earn big paychecks. No one illustrates this more than Stan Lee. Before his death in 2018, his financial worth was estimated at $50 million, according to the website Wealthy Gorilla.

Opportunities for Advancement

Many of the more successful comic book writers also do their own illustrations. Because comics are visual, more attention is usually afforded to the artists. Therefore, comic book writers who take art courses and master some of the key comic book art techniques have more opportunities. In a 2017 article on the Pen & the Pad, writer Marques Williams notes that breaking into the comic book industry can be challenging for writers who do not also draw. He explains that "artists have far more ways of getting recognized and can have very long careers, but writers tend to be phased out after a few years, and generally get paid far less than artists. There are exceptions to the rule . . . but many of the great comic writers are also artists."

What Is the Future Outlook for Comic Book Writers?

According to the BLS, writing jobs will increase by 8 percent through 2026. That is considered average growth for all occupations and translates into another ten thousand jobs.

Since the advent of online books, there has been a steady decline in print publications, but that does not seem to affect comic books. Writer Megan Leonhardt commented on this in a November 2017 article for *Money* magazine: "Marvel and DC Comics are once again facing off in an epic box-office duel this month, with the release of *Thor: Ragnarok* and *Justice League*—two superhero films that, of course, have their roots in the comic book industry. Print isn't dead to this world—the industry makes $800 million-a-year . . . and employs tens of thousands to do so."

There has been an explosion of movie adaptations of popular comics. Buoyed by box office success both at home and abroad, movie producers are looking to the comic book world for their next scripts. Television, too, has been riding this trend with hits such as *The Walking Dead*, based on the zombie apocalypse comic book series by Image. This property is poised to spawn movies and even more television shows.

Find Out More

Authors Guild
31 E. Thirty-Second St., Seventh Floor
New York, NY 10016
website: www.authorsguild.org

The Authors Guild is a national organization for writers. Its website offers information on copyright issues, contracts, finding agents, and self-publishing.

Comic-Con International: San Diego
website: www.comic-con.org

Comic-Con International: San Diego is a nonprofit educational corporation whose goal is to highlight comics and other related art forms, such as fantasy and science fiction, through conventions and events.

National Cartoonists Society (NCS)
website: www.reuben.org

The NCS is an international organization that represents professional cartoonists, including those working with comic books, newspaper comics, animation, and magazine and book illustrations. The NCS publishes a free magazine that features interviews with top cartoonists as well as information on the cartoon and comics industry.

Science Fiction & Fantasy Writers of America (SFWA)
website: www.sfwa.org

The SFWA is an organization for writers, artists, graphic novelists, and other professionals in the fields of science fiction, fantasy, and related genres. Its website provides information on copyright issues, contracts, submitting and protecting work, finding agents, working with editors, and writing tips.

Society of Children's Book Writers and Illustrators (SCBWI)
4727 Wilshire Blvd., Suite 301
Los Angeles, CA 90010
website: www.scbwi.org

The SCBWI is an international organization for writers and illustrators of books for children and young adults. It offers webinars, workshops, and conferences, and its website provides information about grants, copyrights, and contracts.

Comic Book Artist

What Does a Comic Book Artist Do?

Comic book artists are visual storytellers. According to the Art Career Project website, "Artists must . . . be able to tell a story that takes readers (or viewers) on a journey through sequential panels of artwork." Sometimes comic book artists work with a writer, illustrating the writer's script. Other times, the artist is also the writer. Either way, the same article continues, "you still must have a story in mind; from start to finish."

Comic book artists work in a variety of styles, formats, and genres. For example, some specialize in digital painting and others in hand-drawn comics. Formats also vary for this unique art form. The thirty-two-page book format is most common, but comics are also available in book-length versions (graphic novels) that feature an original story or a compilation of many individual issues. Comic book artists might also find themselves creating art for a variety of genres, including thrillers, fantasy, memoirs, or horror.

Regardless of style, format, and genre, the artist's job is to create the visual story for the comic.

At a Glance

Comic Book Artist

Minimum Educational Requirements
Bachelor's degree preferred

Personal Qualities
Advanced art skills; good hand-eye coordination and manual dexterity; great communication skills; good organizational and time-management skills

Working Conditions
Home or studio environment; long hours during deadlines; sitting, mostly at a computer

Salary Range
About $22,000 to more than $101,000*

Number of Jobs
53,400 as of 2016*

Future Job Outlook
Growth of 6 percent through 2026*

*Includes craft and fine artists

This includes developing characters, settings, and action. Artists often do a rough storyboard—a series of sequential drawings—to communicate the vision for the comic book. The artist will then solicit feedback from others working on the project. Once the sketches are approved, the artist does the finished artwork.

In larger publishing houses, there are often several specialized artists for each part of the art process. One might focus on characters or backgrounds, and another might work on cover art. The penciller sketches each scene in pencil. Next, the inker goes over everything in ink, adding shading to create depth. The colorist then comes in and fills all the images with colored ink. And finally, the letterer, a font specialist, fills in the text for the speech balloons and visual sound effects.

Since comic books are a visual medium, the artist's work is often more recognizable in the comic book world than the writer's work. For this reason, most artists display their work on their own websites and on social media. This can help them gain fans, sell their work, or get noticed by a publisher.

How Do You Become a Comic Book Artist?

Education
Comic book artists often do not have formal art education. However, most comic book publishers prefer to hire artists with a bachelor's degree in fine art, sequential art, or illustration. Other areas of study could include studio art, painting, or animation. Courses should include drawing, painting, illustration, anatomy, and digital graphics. Certificates in graphic novel and comic book art can be obtained from some art schools and other institutions with dedicated comic book art programs. These programs might offer courses in both traditional and digital art as well as comic-specific courses in subjects like lettering, panel layout, and color application.

Internships
When hiring artists, most comic book studios prefer at least two years' experience (in addition to a degree). One way to get some

real-world experience is through an internship. Many comic book studios offer internships. Competition is fierce for these positions, which provide experience, industry connections, and potentially a job.

Jeremy Melloul of the blog *Creator at Large* says many comic book creators started out as interns. On his blog, Melloul interviewed Sasha Bassett, who had interned with the comic book company Milkfed Criminal Masterminds in Portland, Oregon. Bassett recalled her internship experience:

> I learned that if I REALLY devoted myself and focused, I could probably make it in the comics industry. Maybe not be a big name, but survive and put out decent work. It's all about keeping on top of lots of small tasks, and making sure people are all on the same page. Those are strengths I already have, and if I had a good team behind me, it seems doable. This kinda took the mystery out of the process and makes it seem like a tangible option I could pursue.

Breaking Into the Business

Some professionals say the best way to break into the comic book business is to get an entry-level job—any job—with a comic book publisher. Even if the position is not an artist's job, the employee can learn about the industry while working toward his or her dream job. An entry-level job at a comic book publisher or animation studio offers relevant experience and puts an artist in the path of art directors and publishers.

Aspiring comic book artists also can create comic strips for their school websites and newspapers as a way to gain experience. They might also consider self-publishing. Although indie publishing can be an expensive enterprise, it can provide experience and sometimes leads to being picked up by a traditional publisher. Artists can also start their own comic-related blog as a way to get industry attention, or they can post their work on comic book websites and blogs. Comic book publishers like DC Comics and Marvel often look for new talent on these sites.

The creative process for a comic book artist often begins with hand-drawn images. The artists create the visual story for the comic. This includes developing characters, settings, and action.

Comic book artists should also attend industry events such as Comic-Con, an international entertainment and comic book convention. Artists can meet art directors and publishers, who often accept art samples or are open to looking at portfolios.

Artists need to promote themselves. They can print high-quality images of their work on postcards and send them to publishers. A strong portfolio is a necessity as well. Artists need to show what they can do both artistically and technically. This is where creativity and originality come in—it is important to develop a unique style or brand. According to the Art Career Project, "You may be able to draw fabulous characters and write amazing copy, but if it looks and sounds the same as last year's comics, your work won't get a second glance. Developing your personal brand can take months or even years, and includes hours and hours of drawing and honing your brand. This is crushingly important if you freelance."

Skills and Personality

Comic book artists need advanced art skills. This job requires a variety of styles and an ability to mimic other artists' styles if working on a team. Comic book artists must be as proficient at drawing the human body as drawing a car; as proficient at drawing with a pencil as with a mouse. They also need great hand-eye coordination as well as manual dexterity.

Good communication skills are also important. Creating comics is a collaborative act, and artists must communicate their vision to a variety of people, including writers, editors, and art directors.

Comic book artists also need good organizational and time-management skills in order to survive in this deadline-driven industry. Missing timelines can affect an artist's reputation and his or her ability to obtain repeat work from a publisher.

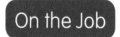

On the Job

Employers

The Bureau of Labor Statistics (BLS) groups craft and fine artists in one occupational category. In 2016 this creative group held 53,400 jobs.

Many comic books are produced by a team of writers and artists at mega publishers such as DC and Marvel. Creator-owned publishers, such as Image Comics, allow for the comics to be created by the individual writers and artists themselves. There are also many smaller, independent comic book publishers. Freelancers can also self-publish their comic books. According to statistics, 66 percent of comic book artists identified as freelance or independent artists.

Working Conditions

Comic book artists primarily work from home offices. Others work in studio environments. And all artists spend a lot of time sitting, often in front of a computer. In a November 2017 article for *Money* magazine on Time.com, Marvel artist Reilly Brown talked about his work as a comic book artist. Brown draws *The Amazing Spider-Man* and other comics. "Keep in mind that while it's usually considered that a comic artist should be able to do a page every day, that is rarely true," Brown says. "Most guys can only do three to four pages per week, and most comic artists work between 10-16 hours a day." Artists put in even longer hours when deadlines loom.

Earnings

The BLS reports that the median annual wage for craft and fine artists (including comic book artists) was more than $49,000 is May 2017. The lowest 10 percent made approximately $22,000, and the highest 10 percent earned more than $101,000.

Comic book artists typically are paid by the project or page, unless they are an employee of a publisher. Pay for comic art varies depending on experience, speed, and the size of the publisher. In the 2017 *Money* article, writer Megan Leonhardt notes that "it's not uncommon for new artists to make $2,000 for a 100-page book. Depending on [how] fast the artist can work, that's only about $2.50 an hour for someone who spends about eight hours working on each page. However, experienced artists who design and execute the cover art can command much higher rates, up to $600 per page at some publishers."

Opportunities for Advancement

The best way for comic book artists to advance in this field is by increasing their art and technology skills. They need to be up to date on industry trends, especially in the area of software.

Comic book artists might also consider taking comic book writing classes if they do not already write. This will enable them to write their own scripts and retain more creative control.

What Is the Future Outlook for Comic Book Artists?

According to the BLS, the craft and fine artists occupational group is projected to grow by 6 percent through 2026. This will add thirty-one hundred jobs to the industry. Statistics show that this is as fast as the average growth for all occupations.

New opportunities for artists continue to appear online with the rise of webcomics. And although print publishing has taken a hit in most areas, comic books are booming. With the string of wildly successful superhero (and superheroine) blockbusters, movie producers are scouring comic books to find their next hot property.

Television is not exempt from this trend, and there are several comic adaptations in the works, including Marvel's new show *Marvel Rising*. The show targets what has been, until recently, an often-ignored market in the comic book industry: girls and young women. Diverse characters are also taking center stage. A desire to tell their stories will lead to more opportunities to break into this intensely competitive market. In a July 2018 article in *Den of Geek* magazine, Sana Amanat, Marvel's vice president of content and character development, talks about Marvel's new emphasis on creating more diverse characters. "Our characters are reflective of that world outside your window," she says, "and they should not only have different points of view and experiences, they should also look like the world outside."

Find Out More

Comic-Con International: San Diego
website: www.comic-con.org

Comic-Con International: San Diego is a nonprofit educational corporation whose goal is to highlight comics and other related art forms, including fantasy and science fiction, through conventions and events.

Graphic Artists Guild
31 W. Thirty-Fourth St., Eighth Floor
New York, NY 10001
website: www.graphicartistsguild.org

The Graphic Artists Guild provides advocacy, community, and resources for graphic artists, interactive designers, illustrators, cartoonists, digital artists, animators, web programmers, and developers. Its website offers webinars as well as information on ethics, pricing work, and contracts.

Science Fiction & Fantasy Writers of America (SFWA)
website: www.sfwa.org

The SFWA is an organization for writers, artists, graphic novelists, and other professionals in the fields of science fiction, fantasy, and other related genres. Its website provides information on copyright issues, contracts, submitting and protecting work, finding agents, working with editors, and writing tips.

Society of Children's Book Writers and Illustrators (SCBWI)
4727 Wilshire Blvd., Suite 301
Los Angeles, CA 90010
website: www.scbwi.org

The SCBWI is an international organization for writers and illustrators of books for children and young adults. It offers webinars, workshops, and conferences, and its website provides information about grants, copyrights, and contracts.

Graphic Novelist

Graphic novels are a unique art form. They are essentially book-length comics, but they combine the elements of literature and visual art to create a cinematic storytelling experience. Graphic novels tell a single narrative that is typically wrapped up by book's end, not unlike a traditional novel. Also, due to their length, they have more room to tell a complex, detailed story that reads more like a novel than a comic book. Yet like comic books, graphic novels tell their stories using sequential art panels that marry both art and text.

Because graphic novels are a cross between comic books and traditional novels, their creation requires a unique mindset and process. Graphic novelist Steve Kissing explains in a July 2018 article on the *Writer's Digest* website, "Through the process of creating my graphic novel, I thought of it less as traditional writing and more like creating a storyboard for a movie, for which I was writing captions. This helped me to 'see' the story in images rather than just words."

Graphic novels may be fiction or nonfiction and cover a wide array of genres, from romance to thrillers to memoirs. They can be targeted at

At a Glance

Graphic Novelist

Minimum Educational Requirements
Bachelor's degree optional

Personal Qualities
Creative; great writing and communication skills; time-management skills

Working Conditions
Most work from home on a computer; long hours when on deadline

Salary Range
About $30,000 to more than $118,000*

Number of Jobs
More than 131,000 as of 2016*

Future Job Outlook
Growth of 8 percent through 2026*

*Includes writers and authors

children, teens, or adults. Those published by literary publishers are typically written by a single author as opposed to a writing team or contract writers, as is often done in the comic book industry. Sometimes the writer is also the illustrator; other times, the writer submits only the manuscript to a publisher and is then partnered with an illustrator. In the latter case, "the script describes the images for the artist to capture in each frame," says Kissing, "while leaving plenty of room for his or her imagination and talent to enhance the scene."

There are many ways to write a graphic novel. Some writers, even those who do not draw, sketch a rough layout or thumbnail sketches (tiny blocks of images) to help them plot the panels. Some write their stories in script form or describe what will happen in each panel, adding captions and written sound effects. Nonfiction writers may need to do research or interview others to create their narrative. Writing a graphic novel is different from writing a regular novel, according to Kissing. "So much of a good story is rooted in how writers describe people, places and things for the reader to see in her mind's eye. With a graphic novel, the visuals do virtually all of that heavy lifting. As such, far fewer words are needed."

Creating a graphic novel is a long process, especially if a person is both the writer and illustrator. Raina Telgemeier adapted several books from the popular children's series the Baby-Sitter's Club into graphic novels. She shares her process in an interview on the website of *Cosmopolitan* magazine:

When an idea is accepted by the publisher, I'll sign a contract and start drawing thumbnails. Then I'll write and sketch 250 pages and then work with my editor on the story. Once everyone is happy—after two to four revisions, which usually takes me about a year—I'll start final artwork.

I use better paper and nicer pencils and ink, and I redraw everything. I pencil first and that takes about half a year. Then I'll ink the book, which is tracing over my pencil lines with permanent ink. That takes four to five months. Then everything gets scanned into a computer and I have a colorist who colors in my work. The text is dropped in by a computer. The whole process takes about two years.

How Do You Become a Graphic Novelist?

Education

Graphic novelists do not necessarily need postsecondary education, but anything that improves their craft can provide more opportunities. Writers might consider a bachelor's degree in English, creative writing, or children's book writing. Illustrators might seek a degree in fine arts, sequential drawing, or illustration. Courses could include life drawing, visual storytelling, or storyboarding.

Since graphic novels have exploded in the traditional publishing industry, many more community colleges and art schools offer associate's degrees or certificates in programs aimed at graphic novelists. Courses might include world building, character design, penciling, lettering, and inking.

Internships

Traditional literary book publishers often offer internships. However, a graphic novelist would find more intern opportunities specific to graphic novels with comic book publishers as they specialize in this art form. Marvel, for example, offers paid internships during the school year in its New York and Los Angeles studios. Even working for a publisher in a noncreative position would help a writer learn the industry and make valuable contacts.

Breaking Into the Business

Unlike comic books, graphic novels are mostly published by literary publishers. Getting published with a traditional literary publisher is always a challenge, whether one writes traditional novels or graphic novels. Although there are some publishers who hire writers for project-based work, the main way to get published is by submitting a manuscript. Some publishers require that an agent submit work on a writer's behalf. Getting an agent is the best way for writers to get their work in front of editors because they have publisher connections. However, sometimes getting an agent is as hard as finding a publisher.

Fortunately, there are other ways a graphic novelist might break into the industry. Many attend conferences for writers and illustrators or comic-specific events such as Comic-Con, an international entertainment and comic book convention. Events like these provide opportunities to meet editors and art directors.

Self-publishing is another option for graphic novelists. It can be expensive, but sometimes it leads to being picked up by a traditional publisher. Most of the publishing costs must be paid up front; however, creators generally keep a larger percentage of the book sales.

Graphic novelists should have a professional-looking website. They need to promote their writing on their sites and on social media platforms in order to gain fans and sell books.

Skills and Personality

Graphic novelists need to be great storytellers, whether they are simply writers or writer-illustrators. They also need to generate original ideas and communicate those ideas both to their readers as well as to their editor and art director.

Writers need to be able to write well. They need to have a good command of the English language, including spelling and grammar rules. Plus, if graphic novelists plan to also illustrate their novels, they will need to have great art skills.

Organizational and time-management skills are also essential. Missing deadlines can affect their reputation and their ability to work with an editor again.

On the Job

Employers

The Bureau of Labor Statistics (BLS) includes graphic novelists under the occupational category of writers and authors. This group held 131,200 jobs in the United States in 2016. Some graphic novelists are employees of comic book publishers, but most work as freelancers. In fact, 64 percent identify as self-employed. Some do writer-for-hire projects, developing and writing a publisher's idea.

67

Working Conditions

With technological advances, graphic novelists can work from anywhere in the world. These professionals typically work from home, which allows them to make their own work schedules. Some stick to a standard workweek, but others work at any hour of the day or night. However, all novelists work long hours when facing a deadline. Plus, being a graphic novelist is a very sedentary job. The majority of the time they are sitting in front of a computer.

Earnings

The median annual wage for writers and authors was about $62,000 per year in 2017, according to the BLS. The lowest 10 percent of people working in this occupational category earned less than $30,000; the highest 10 percent earned more than $118,000.

In the literary publishing world, graphic novelists receive royalties (a percentage of the profits generated by book sales) from their books after they are published. Royalties are split between the writer and the artist. In addition, they often receive an advance, which is a sum of money based on the number of books that the publisher predicts will sell. Money earned through royalties is deducted from the advance until it is paid out.

Some graphic novelists have made a lot of money off their craft. Dav Pilkey, the creator of the Captain Underpants series for children, has been wildly successful as a graphic novelist. According to Scholastic, his publisher, this graphic novel series has sold more than 80 million copies worldwide and has been translated into twenty-eight languages. His 2018 graphic novel, *Dog Man*, sold 13 million copies in just a couple of months.

Pilkey's success, however, is not the norm. Most authors supplement their income with book-related activities like speaking engagements, workshops, and school visits. Some also work full-time or part-time jobs.

Opportunities for Advancement

There is a current trend in literary publishing to publish writer-illustrators as opposed to having a separate writer and illustrator on one project. Being both the illustrator and the writer also allows for more creative control. A writer-illustrator would also earn the full royalty on the book. Thus, it would be beneficial for writers to do their own illustrations.

Book creators often advance in their careers as they publish more books. With every book they gain more fans; once established, they have increased opportunities to sell their manuscripts to more publishers.

What Is the Future Outlook for Graphic Novelists?

According to the BLS, there will be an 8 percent job growth for writers through 2026, resulting in ten thousand more jobs. That is considered average growth for all occupations.

The demand for graphic novels has grown in recent years. They have been turned into movies (such as *Watchmen*) and television series (such as *Gotham*). They have also been adapted from classic literary works—everything from Dickens to Shakespeare. Interest in graphic novels has blossomed among less traditional groups, including women and children. According to the NPD Group, which compiles global book sales data, the comics and graphic novel market experienced 15 percent growth between 2014 and 2017—making it one of the highest growth categories in the traditional publishing industry. On the company's website, industry analyst Kristen McLean explains: "There is a whole new audience emerging for comics and graphic novels; these readers are younger, they are more diverse, and they are getting their books from a much wider range of channels than we typically think of for comics. . . . We have seen this category grow for a few years now, and we have no reason to think it's just a flash in the pan." All of this growth bodes well for those who wish to make this their career.

Find Out More

Authors Guild
31 E. Thirty-Second St., Seventh Floor
New York, NY 10016
website: www.authorsguild.org

The Authors Guild is a national organization for writers. Its website offers information on copyright issues, contracts, finding agents, and self-publishing.

Comic-Con International: San Diego
website: www.comic-con.org

Comic-Con International: San Diego is a nonprofit educational corporation whose goal is to highlight comics and other related art forms, such as fantasy and science fiction, through conventions and events.

Graphic Artists Guild
31 W. Thirty-Fourth St., Eighth Floor
New York, NY 10001
website: www.graphicartistsguild.org

The Graphic Artists Guild provides advocacy, community, and resources for graphic artists, interactive designers, illustrators, cartoonists, digital artists, animators, web programmers, and developers. Its website offers webinars as well as information on ethics, pricing work, and contracts.

Science Fiction & Fantasy Writers of America (SFWA)
website: www.sfwa.org

The SFWA is an organization for writers, artists, graphic novelists, and other professionals in the fields of science fiction, fantasy, and other related genres. Its website provides information on copyright issues, contracts, submitting and protecting work, finding agents, working with editors, and writing tips.

Society of Children's Book Writers and Illustrators (SCBWI)
4727 Wilshire Blvd., Suite 301
Los Angeles, CA 90010
website: www.scbwi.org

The SCBWI is an international organization for writers and illustrators of books for children and young adults. It offers webinars, workshops, and conferences, and its website provides information about grants, copyrights, and contracts.

Interview with a Comic Book Writer and Artist

Eric Shanower is a freelance writer and cartoonist based in Portland, Oregon. Over the last thirty-four years, Shanower has written and illustrated multiple award-winning and *New York Times* best-selling comic books, graphic novels, and children's books. He wrote the graphic novel adaptations of L. Frank Baum's first six Wizard of Oz novels for Marvel Comics and created the *Age of Bronze* comic book series about the Trojan War for Image Comics. Shanower answered questions about his career by email.

Q: Why did you become a comic book writer and artist?

A: I have made up stories and drawn pictures ever since I was a child. I knew when I was young that I wanted to publish my stories and artwork when I grew up. I also loved comic books when I was a child. It took until I was a teenager to realize that becoming a cartoonist was the perfect way to synthesize my love for both writing and drawing. So that's what I decided to do.

Q: How did you break into the comic book business?

A: After high school I attended the Joe Kubert School of Cartoon and Graphic Art in Dover, New Jersey. It concentrates on comics art and graphic design. All of the instructors are working professionals. In school I had to draw a lot, and I got better at it the more I drew. In my final semester of school, I sent out my portfolio to comics publishers and had interviews with editors in comics publishing in New York City. I got my first professional job the day after graduation and my second job the second day after graduation. The jobs didn't continue one per day, but I've had relatively steady work throughout my career.

Q: Can you describe your typical workday?

A: I try to deal with all my email in the morning. Then the rest of the day I'll write at the computer or draw at my drawing table. My studio is in my home, so I don't have to go far to reach work. I usually get to work before noon and quit work soon after midnight. Of course, I take breaks for meals and errands and other tasks demanded by the world outside.

Q: What do you like most about your job?

A: The creativity. It's a great feeling to put my ideas down and watch a world spring to life—a world of characters who are somehow part of me but are also their own personalities. I also love when I'm able to successfully draw the detailed world those characters move in.

Q: What do you like least about your job?

A: Drawing comics takes a long time because one has to draw everything that will communicate the atmosphere, action, and particularities of the story. It's a lot of work and can get tedious.

Q: What personal qualities do you find most valuable for this type of work?

A: Patience and a facility for the tools of the trade acquired with practice. By *facility* I mean knowing how to use the equipment necessary to get the job done, whether it's drawing with a pencil on paper or with a stylus on a screen. Like any other skills, drawing and writing take lots of practice before one can produce work that's of a professional quality, good enough to be paid for. And I never stop practicing really. I can reach certain points of accomplishment, but I'm never finished learning how to write and draw better. I've also got to maintain enough discipline to produce work on a deadline, which means knowing how much work I'm capable of completing in a given amount of time. All of this has taken time and experience to learn. And the only way for anyone to learn it is to sit down and do it—write and draw.

Q: What is the best way to prepare for this type of job?

A: Read lots and lots of comics of all types and styles, both the good and the bad, to gain a fundamental understanding of how comics can communicate and of the techniques for how to put that communication into practice. Write and draw your own comics, even if they're not good enough to show anyone else—the more you practice, the better you'll get. Keep writing and drawing because it takes a lot of practice to become proficient.

Q: What other advice do you have for students who might be interested in this career?

A: It's a sedentary job, so make sure you follow at least a basic exercise program to keep your body working. Learn as much as you can about copyrights and the comics publishing world. If you're hired to work on characters or stories someone else owns, don't become too emotionally involved in the project—if you do, there's a good chance it'll end badly. Know your limitations, but don't be afraid to push yourself to master new things and push your boundaries. Cultivate a professional attitude.

Other Jobs in Animation and Comics

Animation development
manager
Animation director
Animation production
coordinator
Animation technical artist
Animator and narrative
manager
Animator instructor
Art director
Art editor
Artificial intelligence software
developer
Background painter
Character designer
Comic book colorist
Comic book cover artist
Comic book inker
Comic book penciller
Comic concept artist
Facial animator

Interaction designer
Layout artist
Manga artist
Motion graphics artist/video
editor
Motion graphics designer
Shot creator/animator
Software engineer—
gameplay
Storyboard revisionist
Two-dimensional animation
game artist
Three-dimensional animation
game artist
Video artist
Video editor and motion
graphics animator
Visual development artist
Visual effects software
engineer
Webcomic artist

Editor's note: The US Department of Labor's Bureau of Labor Statistics provides information about hundreds of occupations. The agency's *Occupational Outlook Handbook* describes what these jobs entail, the work environment, education and skill requirements, pay, future outlook, and more. The *Occupational Outlook Handbook* may be accessed online at www.bls.gov/ooh.

Index

Picture Credits

About the Author

W.L. Kitts is a professional freelance writer and children's book author who lives in San Diego, California.

THE FEAST OF DEDICATION

ALSO KNOWN AS "HANUKKAH" IN HEBREW

BY YAHNISA LEAH BAHT ISRAEL

THE FEAST OF DEDICATION IS
TO REMEMBER THE STORY OF
OUR FALLEN ANCESTORS

THERE ONCE WAS AN EVIL AND WICKED KING NAMED KING ANTIOCHUS

HE ATTACKED OUR PEOPLE ON OUR HOLY DAY THE SABBATH

THEN CAME JUDAS MACCABAEUS; A WARRIOR CHOSEN BY THE MOST HIGH

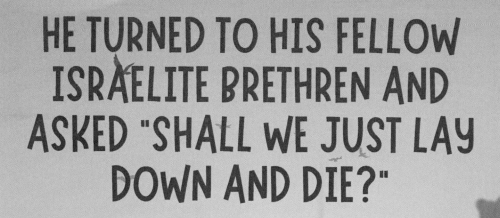

HE TURNED TO HIS FELLOW ISRAELITE BRETHREN AND ASKED "SHALL WE JUST LAY DOWN AND DIE?"

"REMEMBER IN BABYLON, THE BATTLE OF GALATIANS"

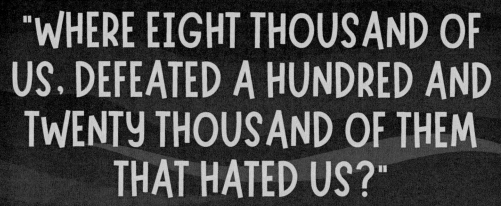

"WHERE EIGHT THOUSAND OF US, DEFEATED A HUNDRED AND TWENTY THOUSAND OF THEM THAT HATED US?"

THEY WERE SIX THOUSAND
AGAINST A MIGHTY ARMY
MUCH MORE THAN THEM

WITH HIS CAPTAINS JOSEPH, JONATHAN, AND SIMON THEY SLEW ABOVE NINE THOUSAND ENEMIES

THEIR FAITH IN YAHWEH LED THEM TO VICTORY!

THE ISRAELITES REBUILT THE TEMPLE, AND WITH VERY LITTLE OIL LIT A CANDLE FOR EIGHT DAYS

AND THE CANDLE LASTED SO LONG BY THE GRACE OF YAHWEH

THE FEAST OF DEDICATION COMMEMORATES THE BRAVERY OF OUR FOREFATHERS

EVERY YEAR WE MUST
REMEMBER THEIR COURAGE IN
OUR HEARTS FOREVER AND
EVER

THE END

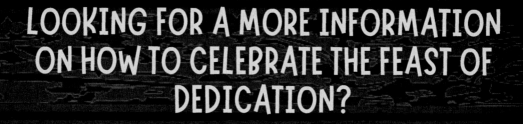

LOOKING FOR A MORE INFORMATION ON HOW TO CELEBRATE THE FEAST OF DEDICATION?

LOOK NO FURTHER!

INSIDE YOU WILL FIND BIBLE VERSES, RECIPES, AND FUN ACTIVITIES ON HOW TO KEEP THE HOLY DAYS OF THE MOST HIGH HERE.

THE HOLY LIBRARIUM

HOLY DAYS

A STEP BY STEP GUIDE
TO CELEBRATING THE HOLY DAYS
IN THE BIBLE

By Yahnisa Leah Baht Israel

Full of recipes, activities for littles and much more!

READ MORE BY YAHNISA LEAH BAHT ISRAEL

THE YHWH SERIES

EARLY LEARNING

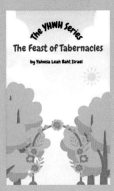

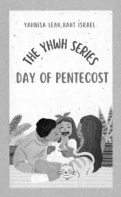

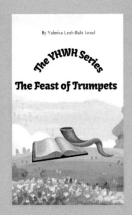

BIBLICAL REFERENCES

2 MACCABEES 8:66-
JOHN 10:22
EZRA 10:9,13
1 KINGS 8:2